tate **publishing**
CHILDREN'S DIVISION

The Master's Tree

Ian A. Bishop

Published by Tate Publishing & Enterprises, LLC
127 E. Trade Center Terrace | Mustang, Oklahoma 73064 USA
1.888.361.9473 | www.tatepublishing.com

Tate Publishing is committed to excellence in the publishing industry. The company reflects the philosophy established by the founders, based on Psalm 68:11,
"The Lord gave the word and great was the company of those who published it."

Book design copyright © 2015 by Tate Publishing, LLC. All rights reserved.
Cover and interior design by Jeffrey Doblados
Illustrations by Sharon DiGangi

Published in the United States of America

ISBN: 978-1-62902-310-6
1. Juvenile Fiction / Religious / Christian / Animals
2. Juvenile Fiction / Religious / Christian / Fantasy
15.01.23

One day, Sparrow was walking through his garden, his favorite thing to do, admiring all of his hard work. The thought of newly grown vegetables for dinner and freshly cut flowers on the table had Sparrow in such a good mood that he began to sing- "Ohhh, the Lord is good to me. So I'll thank the Lord, for giving me the things I need like the sun and the rain and the apple seed, the Lord is good to me…"

As he finished singing his song, he heard a soft and gentle voice calling out to him, "Sparrow!"

In an instant Sparrow was flooded with indescribable joy, making it seem as if he had been sad the moment before. Startled by both the voice and the overwhelming joy, Sparrow looked around for its source. The frightened bird rudely shouted back, "What do you want? Show yourself!"

No sooner did the words leave his lips than he wished they hadn't. It was not as though his joy had left him, but a sudden chilling awe came over him-an odd feeling of standing in the presence of someone exceedingly important. An urge to flee quickly overwhelmed Sparrow.

The voice continued in the same loving tone as before, "Sparrow, my garden has grown well under your caring hands. You have tended it with love and patience, but it lacks one thing to be perfect."

"HIS garden!" Sparrow thought defiantly, "How dare he call my garden, my work, my LIFE, HIS!" However he was still too frightened to say these things aloud and while the thought that his garden was not already perfect angered him even more-his curiosity got the better of him. He needed to know what was missing. " Give me this thing then, sir, so that MY garden can be perfect and I can eat my vegetables in peace and contentment without being bothered by strangers," he added boldly.

"No Sparrow," the voice said, "You must get it for yourself! Fly south as far as your wings can take you. When your strength fails, you will see a tree in another of my gardens tended by my servant. You will know which tree it is by its fruit."

"What type of fruit does it grow, sir?" Sparrow asked with rising excitement.

"Not what type Sparrow, but how many types of fruit."?

"How many types of fruit can this tree grow?" He asked absolutely shaking with anticipation now.

"Twelve types exactly, and if you decide to complete this task and plant the seed of the tree in your garden, I will reward you handsomely."

"I thought the tree was the reward! What could you possibly give me that is greater than a tree that grows twelve different fruits?"

Sparrow asked as his awe increased- that this one offered something greater than the greatest thing he had ever heard.

"The reward of your effort, Sparrow, will be that all of my sons and daughters will honor you for the glory and majesty of this most spectacular of all trees and they will praise it for all time."

"Oh, this is a most wonderful thing," thought Sparrow!

"I must warn you Sparrow, there is one who will try to stop you from getting this seed.

You must not listen to him because his words, no matter how sweet they sound, are lies. My servants are at work all up and down this country, if you should need help do not hesitate to ask. Now farewell, young Mr. Sparrow and remember my warning."

With a flutter of his wings Sparrow set off immediately. The weather being excellent for travel, he set a leisurely pace due south with the sun high above him and the wind whistling in his ears. "What a pleasant time I am having," he thought, "and all that hubbub about evil men and needing help! I shall get there and back again without a bother in the world-and just in time for supper too!"

As the confident bird continued on however, the clouds steadily turned from white to gray and an unpleasant chill began to blow in with the wind. "I should have brought my traveling cloak," he mused as one overly powerful breeze nearly knocked him off course.

The sun steadily became completely blocked out by the blackening clouds overhead and it was all Sparrow could do to keep himself on course. Before long he was being blown wildly to and fro by the violent winds. Out of fear for his life, all thought of finding the right way now gone, he had to dive quickly down into a field of wheat.

No sooner did he set his foot on the ground, than he heard a sound like a rushing train bearing down on him. A tornado had touched down at the other end of the field and was spinning a path of destruction towards Sparrow. With no place left to flee, he started to yell, "help, help me, somebody help!"

At that moment, almost as if out of the ground sprang a tall woman robed from head to foot in a silvery cloak. She threw her cloak over the little bird's body and instantly all fear left him as its cool, silky material brushed against his head. He could still see around him, but instead of the destructive tornado, he saw through her cloak what appeared to be an angry man trudging off in the other direction.

"Oh thank you, thank you!" Sparrow shouted to the woman as she removed her shield from over him. He saw that the sky had now returned to its original peaceful color and the warm breeze had replaced the bone chilling wind of storm.

"You are welcome, Sparrow, but you won't be quite as happy when I tell you that you have been blown completely off course."

"Please my lady, who are you?"

"I am a servant of the Master who sent you on this quest. I tend this field of wheat and all of its inhabitants."

"So this is like your garden then?"

"No, this field belongs to my Master and it is my job to tend it well for Him."

"That must make you angry, doing all that work just so someone else can enjoy it?" "No, Sparrow, for you will find that only work done for others can bring true Joy. Serving my Master is the highest Joy of all. Even if I were to take this field for my own pleasure I would find, within time, that I no longer enjoyed it. Any work done for its sake would only make me like it less."

This gave Sparrow pause to think. "Please, lady of the field, can you point me in the right direction, so I can get the seed and enjoy the praises of others for my magnificent fruit tree?"

"I can," she replied, "you must follow the lower edge of this field until you hit a grove of fruit trees. Do not stop at this grove or you will lose your way again.

Follow on the same path until you see a great tree, in the center of the garden-bigger than them all. This is the tree you seek. Now farewell Sparrow, and do not land again until you see the tree."

After a hearty wave goodbye, Sparrow took off once more following the pathway set out for him. When he reached the end of the wheat field he ached with the effort of flying so far and having gone through so much. As the grove of fruit trees came into sight, every fiber of his being longed for the sweet bite of an apple or pear.

"Maybe I could just take one of these seeds back instead," he thought to himself. "No, I've come this far, and, after all, I have plenty of apples and pears at home. The one who sent me would not be pleased with that!" So he flew on, beyond the point of exhaustion.

Then, just as he thought he could go no farther, a tree like none that he had ever seen, rose before him. "This is it!" he shouted. Landing at the foot of the giant tree, he gazed up in wonder at the many bulging fruits that hung off its branches. His eyes feasted on the blues deeper than the sky, and the yellows brighter than the sun. Even the leaves, translucent, so that the sun shone a radiant green though them, looked like they would be a tasty addition to a salad fit for a king.

"Beautiful isn't it? And enormous," a voice said from behind him.

He whirled around and saw a man with majestic sparkling white robes, a golden crown and a belt around his waist.

Sparrow thought this must be the son of the Master. "Are you a servant of the Master like the lady of the wheat field?" he asked excitedly.

The man let out a hearty laugh that reminded Sparrow oddly of the feel of the chilling wind from the storm. "No, no Sparrow, I am servant to no one, but a lord in my own right. I tend nobody's garden but my own."

Sparrow hesitated, "But the lady said there is no Joy in that."

The man laughed again, "of course she would say that, having never tasted fruit of her own. She wouldn't know the pleasure of doing things on your own, for yourself-despite what others think. But come Sparrow, you are not like her. You know the pleasures of having your own way, of being your own man, so to speak? So I ask you to think, what would planting such a tree as this in your garden do to all your other plants? Can't you see the Master's tree would crowd out all of your vegetables and flowers-leaving only His tree?"

Sparrow replied, "As to your first point, before this day I had always thought that having my own way was the highest pleasure and being master of my own garden was my only desire. But after seeing the lady of the wheat field, and with what Joy she tends it for her Master and His other servants, I have decided that I would rather have her Joy than my pleasures. As to what will happen to my own plants when I plant the Master's tree, I can only say that He has led me this far and he has given me every reason to trust Him. Therefore, I will plant this seed in my garden."

As the last words left his mouth, the man no longer looked majestic in his golden crown and belt-which now looked rather cumbersome, but instead looked horrible to behold! Sparrow instantly recognized him as the man in the field he saw through the lady's cloak.

"You!" he shouted, "you tried to blow me off course before and now you're trying to stop me from getting the seed that I was sent to get!"

The wicked man reached forward to grab Sparrow just as another man, much taller and more plainly dressed, stepped out from behind the tree and stopped the evildoer.

"Leave this place now!" He yelled at Sparrow's attacker.

The wicked man shot one last angry grimace at the little bird before blowing away like a tornado in a blast.

"Welcome at last, Sparrow,' the man said as his face turned to him beaming with delight.

"Thank you, kind sir for helping me. You must be one of the Master's servants?"

"That I am, and that one who tried to stop you was he who the Master warned you about- the one who always tells lies."Looking ashamed, Sparrow replied, "I should have been ready for him. The Master knew he would try to stop me, but I didn't pay heed to his warnings!"

"It is all right little one, what matters is that you didn't listen to him."

"Now here is the seed that you seek. Take and eat one of the twelve pieces of fruit, so that you can renew your strength for your journey home."

Sparrow looked down at the fruit's deep purple coloring, which was like the robes of a king. He tossed it into his thirsty mouth. The richness of the juice bursting through his lips was like a mouthful of warm honey.

A feeling of strength poured into his body and out to his wings- making him feel like he had just awakened from a long satisfying sleep.

"Farewell, Sparrow, the wicked one will not bother you on the journey back as long as you stop for nothing!"

Sparrow tried to say "thanks" but with his mouth full of juice from the fruit all he could do was wave and smile as he flew away. Immediately he felt strength like never before in his wings. He knew that the trip home would be as nothing compared to the journey there.

He flew quickly past the orchard and made it to the wheat field. A moment's temptation to stop to see the lady of the field floated through his thoughts. "No", he said, fighting the urge. "I've learned my lesson to listen to warnings from the Master. No stops until I'm home!"

After a few hours of flight, Sparrow landed with relief just outside his house. He rustled his tail feathers in joy and leapt into the air giving a chirp of victory. "Master, Master!" he yelled, looking around his garden for the master that he had never yet seen. "He's not here," thought Sparrow. "Well, I suppose I should plant the seed so that He can see it sprout when he returns."

But as Sparrow looked around the garden that he loved so much with its beans and cabbage and carrots and flowers patches, he remembered the words of the wicked man and began to despair. "Oh, that man was right", he wailed, "the tree this seed came from was so exceedingly large my plants will all wither and die in its shadow. Yet I trust the Master, that he is good, his plans have not failed me so far." But all the same, Sparrow wept miserably as he planted the seed in the middle of his garden.

Every day after that, Sparrow dutifully watered the ground around the seed until a small green shoot could be seen poking out of the brownish green earth. Sparrow threw himself on the ground crying pitifully at the sight of the baby tree, knowing it spelled the doom of all his other labors. Still he carried on, tending it...day after day... year after year. As great as the beauty of the tree was, the larger it grew, less and less land was left for his precious vegetables. He stopped planting cabbage first, then beans, then carrots...and flowers and squash...and lettuce and peas and peppers... and radishes and cucumbers and broccoli... Until finally all that was left was one single potato.

Sparrow picked the potato one evening, knowing it would be the last he ever grew. He tenderly prepared it for his supper, boiling it and letting butter melt on top of it. With tears in his eyes, he prepared to eat his supper, when suddenly a noise out in his garden startled him.

Sparrow ran to the window and saw to his utter horror, the wicked man standing with two other men beside the great tree. He was no longer dressed like a prince, but like a soldier with a great red plume on his helmet and bronze armor on his chest. One of the other men had an axe in his hand and was eagerly inspecting the tree.

"This is the one, cut it down," the wicked man commanded.

A wave of panic flooded Sparrow's heart. The tree had not even begun to produce fruit, so he would never be able to replant it. He wanted to rush out and yell at the men but he remembered his last encounter with the wicked man. He was not too keen to have another battle.

He watched, tears streaming down his eyes, as the man began to chop down his precious tree-the last thing in his garden-the thing for which his entire garden was destroyed. With each blow of the axe, Sparrow fell deeper and deeper into his chair, until finally with a loud CRACK, the tree was toppled.

The men began to drag the tree away while Sparrow sat crying- something inside of him told him to follow the men. So he got up and snuck quietly behind them as they carried the tree to a barren hillside outside a city.

He saw them strip the tree of its limbs and bark. Next, he watched as they split the truck into six different logs, some longer, some shorter.

"Maybe," thought Sparrow, "the Master wanted to make something out of this tree and he told these men to do it." Even as he thought it, he doubted it, knowing that the wicked man would never do anything for the Master- but still he hoped.

Night fell and the men left, but Sparrow stayed watching through the darkness, hoping to catch a glimpse of the Master. What would become of his tree?

At the rising of the sun, he saw the soldiers return and begin nailing the shorter logs to the longer ones, taking the shape of a cross. They took one of these crosses down the hill and laid the other two flat on the ground.

A short while later, three men were led up the hill, one of them carrying the logs on his back. He witnessed the soldiers beating and spitting on the three men as they made their way towards his logs. A sinking feeling in Sparrow's stomach made his knees shake as he saw the soldiers nail the three men to his logs and raise them up in the air.

"Oh no!" Sparrow wailed, "All my work has ended in this! How terrible that my tree was made to do such a thing as this! Oh where is the Master now, if only he could see his children suffering like this on crosses made out of his tree!" Sparrow, too weak to move now, stood watching as the men suffered and the people underneath them wailed with distress.

Finally, as the men died, Sparrow watched as they were taken down. Two of the men were thrown into a pit like old rags, but those around his body were treating the one who had carried his cross tenderly.

Sparrow stared as they took him away to a great tomb. Placing his body inside the tomb, they rolled a giant stone in front of it.

Sparrow stayed at the tomb as night fell. He wept long into the night until sleep erased his misery. All the next day he sat beside the tomb, head in knees, wandering what it could mean.

He had trusted the Master's plan, trusted that He would somehow look after him because of the tree. "How," he wondered for the hundredth time that day, "how could this have happened?" The weight of Sparrow's grief was too much and he fell into a deep sleep yet again.

The next morning he was awakened, by a loud rumbling sound. Startled from the noise, he jumped up and looked around.

To his utter amazement, the stone blocking the tomb was rolled aside and the man who had hung on the cross was standing before him- shining radiantly in the purest of white robes.

He looked as if he had just stepped out of the wealthiest of all palaces, instead of a hillside tomb. The glory that shown about him made Sparrow look away and yet long to look back all the more.

"Sir, what can it mean?" gasped Sparrow, his trembling wings now covering his eyes.

"It means, Sparrow, that you have done what my Father asked of you."

Sparrow gasped and lowered his wings, "The Master's Son!" The smile that met his eyes when Sparrow looked upon his face wiped away all the sorrow of the past three days. His heart was filled with an overwhelming love for the Master. "But what does it mean, sir, your Father said that all of His children would praise me for the tree. Instead it was cut down and used for the wicked man's purposes?"

"He did not lie Sparrow, all of His children will praise you for your tree, since it became the doorway to His house that all His children might live with Him. They will be forever grateful for the work that you have done in tenderly caring for my tree. I watched you all those years as you watered the tree knowing it meant the death of all your plants.

I cried with you as you wept over the loss of your vegetables and flowers. I knew how hard it would be for you, but in spite of all the pain and doubt you remained faithful to the end. So, as your reward, I will allow you to tend a very special garden, one that no one has ever yet seen but myself and my Father."

"Where is this garden, my Lord?" Sparrow asked, absolutely giddy with Joy.

"It is within my house, the one my children can now come into, thanks to your tree becoming my cross. "Sparrow ," His smile widened as He continued, "In this garden grows a tree, the seeds of which fathered the tree from which your own seed came. It is your tree's grandfather and it is much, much greater than either of the two that you have seen. In fact, it is so great that a river flows through the middle of it, and you will be charged with tending it, so that all of my brothers and sisters can enjoy it when they come home.

"Oh, my Lord, this task is too large for me alone, how will I ever manage such a great tree when I could barely handle my little garden?" Sparrow lamented.

"But Sparrow, you will not be alone in this task. My servants from the wheat field and the orchard will work with you," as he said this, Sparrow looked around and saw the majestic woman in her silvery silken cloak and the humbly dressed man from the orchard appear, both smiling down at him.

"Come along Sparrow," the woman said cheerfully,

"together we will tend the Master's tree for all others to enjoy, and in their Joy, we will find ours as well."

Sparrow followed them as they twirled upward in a windy gust, fast as lightning it seemed, only looking down in time to see the Master's Son smiling up at him before disappearing out of sight.

When he looked back up he gasped as he saw before him the tree that the Master's Son had described, towering above him, its top out of sight. Giant fruits the size of bowling balls bowed the branches, making the fruit of the tree from the other garden seem small in comparison. Even the leaves seemed a richer hue, casting sparkling green lights down on the lazily moving river flowing through the middle of its trunk.

The thought of the pleasure he would have in living and tending the tree with his

two best friends overwhelmed him, making his heart flutter with Joy.

"All the misery that I suffered to get to this place cannot even compare to the Joy that I have now that I am here. I was surely right to trust the Master. He is indeed good, in fact, the best of all!" Sparrow said within his heart.

As the three stood before the great tree breathing in its beauty, a man robed in white could be seen walking toward them from a distance. "Look," shouted Sparrow, "The first of the Master's children has arrived!"

The three ran to welcome him. Sparrow recognized

him as one of the men nailed to the crosses beside the Master's Son.

"Welcome child of the Most High Master, who is Lord of the tree of the twelve fruits, welcome to His everlasting home," the humbly dressed man said in words worthy of the welcome of his Master's first child to come home.

"How came you to be the first to come home?" The lady of the wheat field asked him.

"I hung on the cross to the left of my Master and begged that He would remember me when He came into His kingdom. He promised me that I would be with Him here in paradise and His promises have not failed!"

Sparrow noticed that the man, although dressed in robes of dazzling white, looked ragged in his weather-beaten face. An idea came to him to feed this man one of the great fruits of the tree. So he picked a light-blue gourd-shaped fruit from a low-lying branch and gave it to the man saying, "this is fruit from the Master's tree, all His children have a right to eat of it and share in its pleasures together."

The man's eyes widened as he looked upon the fruit that glowed from within as he touched it.

With a loud crunch, he took a large bite and chewed noisily, laughing all the while. As the juices dripped down his beard, his face looked younger. Lines etched on his face smoothed out, his graying hair thickened and became a flowing golden mane.

The transformation seemed to move down his body as his shoulders lost their slouch and he stood tall before them. He was still laughing, although now less like an old man and more like a child laughing for sheer pleasure.

The other three joined in and only returned to silence when the man finished eating.

"Now that you are fed, the Master has requested your presence in His house." The woman gestured farther up river deeper in the city, and without looking back the man ran forward, his face aglow with Joy.

Sparrow felt such a deep contentment at being able to share the fruit with the man that he finally understood the meaning behind the lady of the wheat field's words about the Joy of serving others. He realized, with a shudder, that the wicked man's ideas must lead to the exact opposite of the Joy he now felt.

As the man disappeared from sight, Sparrow asked his two companions, "what now?"

Before the lady of the field could respond, she said, "Look, another son and a daughter too!"

Sparrow turned around quickly and saw two people coming towards the doorway looking older and more worn than any he had ever seen. "These two must have been waiting for a very long time indeed. The man's beard is trailing behind him! Well, looks like we will need some really big fruit for these two!"

So Sparrow and his friends fed the two and sent them on to the Master. They continued to do the same for all the weary sons and daughters of the Master who made their way to His home.

And so shall they ever do until the very last child is welcomed home and the great banquet begins that will have no end.